Please return/renew this item by the last date shown.
Library items may also be renewed by phone on
030 33 33 1234 (24hours) or via our website

www.cumbria.gov.uk/libraries

Cumbria Libraries

CLIC
Interactive Catalogue

Ask for a CLIC password

Going Batty

John Agard

With illustrations by
Michael Broad

Barrington Stoke

First published in 2016 in Great Britain by
Barrington Stoke Ltd
18 Walker Street, Edinburgh, EH3 7LP

www.barringtonstoke.co.uk

A CIP catalogue record for this book is available
from the British Library upon request

ISBN: 978-1-78112-531-1

Printed in China by Leo

Contents

Chapter 1
Up to No Good

Shona hated bats.

She didn't hate all forms of creepy-crawlies. She loved the feel of ladybirds on her fingers. That felt like summer had sprouted tiny spotted wings in the palm of her hand.

And when Shona helped her grandmother in the garden, she would put on rubber gloves and pick off all those slugs that made their yucky trail up Granny's pots of herbs. Granny grew rosemary, bay leaf, marjoram, lemon balm, chamomile, and all sorts of strange herbs that sat like bursts of green on the concrete slabs in their back garden.

And once in a blue moon, Shona's dad would get into one of his fishing moods. Then he'd dig out his gear from the shed and Shona would be at his side with a tub of earthworms she herself had collected.

Even spiders she could live with, as long as those 8-leggers stuck to the corner and stayed out of the bath.

But bats? Bats were a no-no!

"Hate" was a strong word to Shona's ears, but somehow the word "dislike" didn't get to the bottom of her feelings. Horrid, night-time beasties with their fluttery mouse-heads!

Yes, the plain and simple truth was that Shona hated the sight of bats. To her, they seemed spooky and up to no good.

To cut a long story short, she'd rather aliens invaded Planet Earth than face bats in any shape or form.

Chapter 2
A Flying Visit

The last thing Shona was expecting was a surprise visit from a member of the fruit bat clan. Some people called them flying foxes. Shona felt this was a bit of an insult to the beauty of real, red-coated foxes.

It was one of those hot evenings that sometimes come along in late September and make some born-and-bred Brits moan about the heat. If it's not too cold then it's "a bit too hot for this time of year".

But Shona's dad was from the Caribbean, and he was in his element.

"Not exactly Montserrat heat," he said, and winked. "But I'm not complaining. This heatwave spell can last until December, that's fine by me!"

And for all Shona's mum was half Irish, she also seemed at home in the British weather. She loved those warm Septembers people call an "Indian summer". But she called them "Nigerian summers", since she was half Nigerian too.

For her, the late sunshine burst was a summer bonus in the middle of autumn. Autumn was her favourite season, when the trees showed off their top-of-the-range golden browns.

Shona's granny had moved from Montserrat to live with them. She was always happy to see the sun smile from London's grey skies, but she liked the snow too. It never snowed in Montserrat and so real snow still held a sort of fairy-tale magic.

"I come all this way and you mean to tell me, I'm still waiting to see a proper white Christmas?" she would say. "I want the snow, the one-horse open sleigh, the Robin Redbreast, the everything!"

"Global warming, Mums," Shona's dad would say to tease her. "A white Christmas might soon be a thing of the past. At this rate, it'll be barbecue weather in the middle of December, don't you worry."

But Jack Frost was a long way away on that sweltering September evening.

They were enjoying a quiet family night-in with the windows open. Shona sat on a stool between her mum's knees while Mum plaited her hair. Dad was lost in some endless cricket

match on the telly. Granny nodded in her
chair, a bundle of knitting on her lap.

But this cosy family scene was about to be interrupted.

At first it sounded like a tennis ball. Perhaps the boy from next door had tossed it in the open window.

But tennis balls don't make squeaky noises like an out-of-tune violin.

And tennis balls don't have wings and fangs like a mini blood-sucking Dracula.

Chapter 3
On the Ceiling

Shona knew what her dad was like and so, when he shouted out "Bat!", she thought he must be fooling around.

It wasn't the first time he'd reached for the cricket bat he kept in a corner of the living room. This bat was a souvenir from his days playing cricket as a small boy back in Montserrat, when he dreamed about opening the batting for the West Indies.

Now the bat stood there, like a piece of sculpture from the past, until the cricket was on and Dad decided to strike a pose in front of the telly. "Hook, sweep, cover, drive ..." These were the words he'd use for his make-believe shots.

But that night when he shouted "Bat!", Shona could hear a chill in his voice.

"Bat!" he said again, this time in a whisper, with a finger to his lips.

Mum left off plaiting Shona's hair, made a dash for the kitchen and returned to the living room with a broom. She waved it as if she was a Samurai warrior.

"Where's the little devil?" she asked, and raised the broom like a weapon.

"There, by the curtains ..." Dad said.

"Where by the curtains?" asked Mum.

"No, there by the picture ..." Dad said.

"Where by the picture?"

Then Shona heard herself scream –

"On the ceiling!"

A scream so chilling that next door must have thought a horror movie was in progress.

She looked up to see the small flying mammal with its wings folded around it. It looked for all the world like it had pitched a little tent against the ceiling!

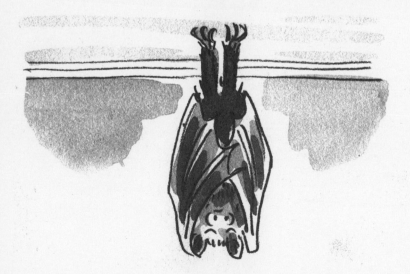

By then, Shona had made a beeline for cover behind the sofa. She pulled a couple of cushions over her head. She'd heard that bats liked landing in people's hair and she didn't fancy a little furry demon for a hairdresser.

"How about we turn off all the lights?" Mum said. "I saw a TV programme that said bats will make for the outside lights if the inside lights are off."

Shona hoped Mum had got that right, and that it wasn't the case that bats preferred to zoom in on humans huddling in the dark.

"What's wrong with the lights?" Granny asked, as she woke up from her nap. "Don't tell me we're having a black-out? London getting like the Caribbean!"

"Shush!" Mum said. "There's a bat in the house! Somehow or other, it flew in."

"And somehow or other, it will fly out," was all the comfort Granny could offer.

They crouched in the dark for what seemed like a hundred years as their hearts pounded at the circling and swooping of their unwelcome guest.

Then Granny said, "Told you it would find a way out. The bat's not stupid. Who'd want to hang around near a couple of maniacs with cricket bat and broomstick!"

Then Granny added in a faraway voice, "Might even have been a visitor from the other side. The dead keep an eye on the living."

Shona's mum and dad laughed, but Shona didn't. "Now you're scaring me," she said.

That night Shona didn't go to bed until they had searched every corner of the living room. The folds of the curtains. The backs of pictures. Behind the bookcases. Under the sofa.

And when her mum had finished plaiting her hair, Shona insisted on sleeping in a woolly hat. Now she hated bats more than ever.

Chapter 4
Make Friends

This was Shona's first day back at school after half-term and she couldn't wait to tell everyone about her bat adventure. Her English teacher, Miss Bates, always asked the class to report any special news from their holidays.

English was Shona's favourite subject and Miss Bates was her favourite teacher. At first the class didn't quite know what to make of Miss Bates, who said they could call her Luana.

She said she was named Luana after her Brazilian grandmother.

"Sorry to disappoint you all," she added. "But I'm not into football and I don't drink coffee. Nothing like a nice cup of tea."

Shona thought Luana was a good name. With her very black hair and very black glasses, she also thought Miss Bates would make a very good Goth. Yes, Shona could well imagine her with velvet dark lipstick and inky dark fingernails.

Miss Bates was always reading poems to the class. Not just reading, but saying them out loud by heart. Amazing how she could say all those words from memory. Like rhyming magic coming out of her mouth!

So it wasn't in any way strange that she should welcome them back with a smile and a sudden burst of poetry.

"Twinkle twinkle little bat
How I wonder what you're at
Up above the world you fly
Like a tea-tray in the sky."

But what Shona did find strange was that out of all the poems in the world, why did Miss Bates choose one about bats? Shona recognised it from *Alice's Adventures in Wonderland*, and she always thought it was funny. But somehow today she didn't find it funny. More like a spooky coincidence.

Then Miss Bates shared out two stacks of bright yellow cards with bold black letters on the back.

When Shona turned over the first yellow card, she nearly had a fit. Were the words for real? Or was she seeing things?

PUT ASIDE YOUR PREJUDICE.
MAKE FRIENDS WITH A BAT.

"Coincidence" was the word that again came to Shona's mind. Her dad always said, "There's no such thing as coincidence, everything happens for a reason." But coincidence would have to do. Yes, what a coincidence!

She hesitated to turn over the other yellow card. When at last she did, she saw four words printed in bold letters.

Ugly
Adorable
Helpful
Destructive

Then Miss Bates said, "Which two of these adjectives do you think best describe bats?"

Of course, the question was a no-brainer, but somebody at the back of the class wanted to check.

"Is it a trick question, Miss?" they asked. "Like a brain teaser?"

Miss Bates peered over her glasses. "Not a brain teaser," she said. "More like a heart prober."

Without too much brain pain, the whole class agreed that bats were "ugly". And "destructive". To put it mildly.

"What if I said bats are adorable and helpful to the environment?" Miss Bates asked. "What if I said they are a blessing to the eco-system?"

"We'd say you can't be serious, Miss!" the class chanted.

"And what if I said I was never more serious in all my life? Bats have been given a bad name, a bad press, a bad everything. If bats could go to court, they'd sue humans for defamation of character."

Shona was tempted to relate her encounter with the bat in their house, but something held her back. The mere thought of that horrible moment gave her the creeps.

Chapter 5
Too Many Vampire Movies

Miss Bates had only just got going on the subject of bats.

"Last term we looked at Neanderthals and discovered that they weren't quite the brainless cave-dwellers we thought," she said. "Now I'd like us to take a closer look at bats."

"They're proper nasty, Miss," someone shouted.

"You lot have been watching too many vampire movies, that's what," Miss Bates said. "Who's scared of bats? Hands up!"

Not a hand went up.

"Just as well," Miss Bates said with a smile. "But lots of people are. And the best way to deal with your fear is to embrace it. Bats live in a twilight world, and they are unfamiliar and unknown. And when we don't understand a thing, we fear it. It's time to reconsider these cute little creatures ..."

Shona couldn't believe her ears. Did Miss Bates just say "cute"? Wasn't this going a wee bit too far?

"But don't they suck blood and give people rabies, Miss?" another voice asked.

"A myth," Miss Bates said. "There's more chance of getting rabies from a dog than a bat." She went on to tell them how most bats eat insects and fruit. Only vampire bats like blood, she said, and even they prefer the blood of horses and pigs. And then she explained how bats use sound echoes to find their way in the dark.

"But don't they get tangled up in people's hair?" Shona asked, as she thought back to that bat flitting about their living room.

"Don't worry, Shona," Miss Bates said. "Bats are not out to mess up your hairstyle. They are too clever for that. They'll avoid your head and make for the nearest door."

Then Ewa blurted out, "My grandmother says that in Poland bats bring good luck."

"That's very interesting, Ewa," Miss Bates said. "For the Chinese, too, the bat is a symbol of good luck. In fact, the same character can mean 'bat' and 'blessing'."

"My granny from Montserrat says that bats might be the souls of the dead come to pay the living a visit," said Shona, inspired by Ewa, her new-found friend.

"Good on your granny," Miss Bates said. "She's in the company of the ancient people of Babylon, who also saw bats as spirits visiting from the beyond."

That was the moment Shona came out with, "We had a visitor last night, Miss."

"A visitor from the Caribbean or a visitor from the beyond?" Miss Bates said with a laugh.

"No, Miss, the visitor was a big scary bat. Zooming round like crazy in our living room ..."

Just then the bell sounded for lunch, which meant Shona would have to save her bat story for later.

Or so she thought.

But on her way out, Miss Bates, all excited, whispered, "A moment, Shona, please. I'm dying to hear more about this bat in your living room."

Chapter 6
How Close Is Close

Shona didn't know where to start.

So she set the scene by telling Miss Bates how her mum had been plaiting her hair, her granny in her chair knitting, her dad watching cricket on the telly, and then a sudden noise. Something had flown into the curtains.

"Next thing, Dad was armed with a cricket bat and Mum with a broom ..."

"And what about you, Shona?" Miss Bates laughed. "Were you armed with your brolly?"

Shona saw herself brandishing a brolly, beside her dad and mum with bat and broom. That made her think of the three musketeers, and made her smile. But she was serious as she told Miss Bates about their encounter with the bat.

"It was kind of spooky, Miss," she said. "We were there in the dark, waiting, waiting ... and I screamed like a horror movie ... but the bat must have gone out the way it came ... just like Granny said it would ... but I still went to sleep in a hat. I just hate the sight of bats, and I don't trust their hair-dressing skills."

"Oh Shona, you do make me laugh," Miss Bates said. "Might it just have been a young bat that had got separated from its parents? Sometimes a young one does get lost. Did your mum and dad check the fireplace?"

"We don't have a fireplace, Miss. But we checked behind the radiators. And behind the curtains ... and behind the pictures ..."

"What about the airing cupboard? Did you check the airing cupboard?" Miss Bates asked.

"The airing cupboard? No, Miss."

"What about the outside window sills? Did you check them for bat droppings?"

"I wouldn't know what bat droppings look like, Miss."

Shona thought Miss Bates sounded more like a detective than a teacher. There was no stopping her.

What was all this about bat droppings? A bat whizzing around the living room is one thing. But bat poo? Yuk! That's another matter.

Then Miss Bates leaned closer. "It's not the end of the world, Shona," she said. "Don't look so worried. I'll let you into a secret. I belong to a Bat Conservation group. We go on bat-spotting walks round the parks and canals. It's great fun. And isn't it a nice bit of serendipity that a bat flew into your house just last night, and here we are today, starting a project on bats?"

"Serendipity, Miss, is it like coincidence?" Shona couldn't help asking.

"More than coincidence. More like parallel magical connections. Events coming together in an uncanny way. Almost supernatural, if you ask me."

Then Shona spotted the word BATES, in Miss Bates's neat handwriting on a notebook. All of a sudden she realised that the name contained BATS …

"Bats!" she almost shouted. "Look, Miss, the name BATES contains BATS!"

"Well spotted, Shona," Miss Bates said. "Now how about that for serendipity? It's like spotting a fossil in a word. And you could say I'm batty about bats! Tell you what. Why don't I pop round later this evening with my bat detector? Who knows – there may be a colony of bats closer than you think."

'But how close is close?' Shona thought, as she and Ewa walked home from school that day.

Chapter 7
The Attic

Miss Bates turned up at Shona's door in a hoody and leggings. True to her word, she was armed with an odd device, which they took to be her bat detector.

"Brilliant," she said when Granny offered her a brew of lemon balm from her own herb garden. "Thank you so much."

Miss Bates sipped her lemon balm and asked Shona's mum and dad what they had been up to of late.

"How's the acting?" she asked.

"I've tried out for the part of the wicked Snow Queen in the panto at Hackney Empire," said Shona's mum. "Shona's granny would be over the moon if I got it, because she's obsessed with snow, aren't you, Mums?"

"Ignore her, Miss Bates," Granny said in a dry voice.

"Mum will make a wicked Snow Queen," Shona teased.

"I'll take that as a compliment, shall I?" Shona's mum laughed.

Then Miss Bates turned to Shona's dad. "And how's the painting going?"

"Still battling with the blank canvas," Shona's dad said, with a smile. "This artist life isn't easy. One per cent inspiration, 99 per cent perspiration."

"Dedication, that's the word," Miss Bates replied. "But, gosh, this September is so hot! Don't mind if I disrobe?" Miss Bates took off her hoody. Under it she had on a pink top, and on her left shoulder Shona saw a tattoo of a bat hovering over some Chinese writing.

"What does it say?" Shona's mum asked.

Miss Bates turned to Shona. "Come on, Shona, what does it mean? Remember I told you in class today?"

"Um ..." Shona said. "Does it mean 'bat' and 'good fortune'?"

"Well done, Shona. Knew I could depend on you."

"Is it a real one?" Shona's dad asked.

"You mean the tattoo or my bat detector?" said Miss Bates. "The short answer is yes, both are real."

"I myself have played with the idea of a tattoo," Shona's mum admitted for the first time. "In fact, two tattoos. Little ones, mind you. A harp for my Irish roots and a talking drum for my Nigerian roots. How about that, Sir Garfield? Fancy seeing me in tattoos?"

Mum always called Dad "Sir Garfield" when she wanted to put him on the spot.

"Better you than me," Shona's dad said. "I keep well clear of needles, even knitting needles. Is that not true, Mums?"

Granny just smiled and carried on knitting.

Then Miss Bates switched to her detective mode and got down to the matter in hand.

"Lovely cup of tea, Granny, and nice chatting with you guys," she said. "But I'm afraid we must return to the B-word – Bats. Shona said that you've had a visit from one of our furry friends. She also said you had a good look around the living room to make sure it had gone. I'm sure it has, but I thought I'd have a nose-around anyhow, if that's all right with you?"

"Go right ahead."

They all followed Miss Bates into the back garden, except for Granny, who was too comfy in her chair.

"Ah, don't you just love the smell of chamomile?" Miss Bates said. She breathed in the scent from Granny's endless pots of herbs as she made her way to the window sills.

Then Miss Bates cried, "Bingo! Just as I suspected. Guano!"

"Guano?" Shona said.

"Bat ... droppings, to put it politely," Miss Bates explained. "Excellent fertiliser."

Then, she said, "Look, do you see that? Undigested insects. Most likely flies. Bats save farmers a lot of dosh. The more bats around, the less they have to fork out for pesticides. And the environment could do without more chemicals."

"You're a real bat expert, Miss Bates,"
Shona's mum said.

"True," Miss Bates said. "But please just call me Luana. Some of my close friends even call me Loony Lu. But that's friends for you!"

Then Shona chipped in. "Miss Bates was named after her Brazilian granny. Perhaps 'Bates' is her name from her English dad."

"You're right, Shona." Miss Bates laughed. "Perhaps that explains everything!"

"How strange," Shona's mum said. "I'm named Brigid after my grandmother. She was Irish, you see, and my dad's side of the family is Nigerian."

Dad didn't want to be left out. "Mums named me after Sir Garfield Sobers," he said. "He was a Barbados cricket legend. Old as she is, she still likes her cricket, don't you, Mums?"

Granny had good hearing. "Who you calling old?" she shouted from inside. "Watch your mouth, you Mister Garfield!"

Miss Bates smiled. "Well, here we have all the world under one roof!" she said. "Speaking of which, have you checked the attic?"

"The attic?" everyone else chimed in together.

Chapter 8
A Colony

On their way to the attic, Miss Bates stopped.

"Mind if I nose around the airing cupboard?" she asked.

"Let me give you a hand with those quilts and what not," Shona's dad offered. He grabbed a bundle of quilts and a couple of laundry bags bursting with winter clothes.

"Oh you poor thing!" Miss Bates said. Dad
looked surprised. "No, I don't mean you,
Garfield," she said. "I'm referring to that
darling in the corner there. A baby bat. Dead
from over-heating no doubt. We'll bury it in
the garden and have a little service, shall we?"

Shona's mum and dad were lost for words
when Miss Bates held the bat in her bare hands
and asked for a towel to wrap the "sweet little
creature" up in.

"Now the moment of truth has arrived," she said.

She winked at them all as she moved her bat detector around the top of the airing cupboard.

"I'm picking up some squeaks and clicks all right," she told them. "Bats give off sounds too high-pitched for the human ear to hear. This device here lets us mortals pick up those sounds. And I reckon you have a colony in your attic."

"A colony, you say?" Shona's dad asked with a twinkle in his eye. Shona groaned – she knew where this joke was going. "I hope it ain't Christopher Columbus come back as a bat to colonise our attic!"

"I think you've got that the wrong way round." Miss Bates laughed. "The bats are more likely to colonise Columbus!"

"Garfield forgets to shut the window," Shona's mum said. "The attic is where he paints, and stores all his junk ..."

"Junk? Memorabilia, if you please," Shona's dad said.

Miss Bates winked at Shona's mum. "Well," she said, "here's Garfield's big chance to de-clutter that junk. Amazing how good it is for the mind to de-clutter."

"Mind your head," was Shona's dad's reply, as Miss Bates dodged a dodgy crossbeam to nimble her way up into the attic.

Before they were all up the ladder, they could hear Miss Bates going "ooh" and "aah".

"There's your answer," she declared. "A colony of pipistrelles. They must be after a place to spend the winter. Aren't they adorable?"

Miss Bates pointed her torch into a corner stuffed with bits of carpet, left-over cork tiles, rolls of wallpaper and all sorts of junk.

Yes, there they were – a roost of little bats hanging from the beams of the musty corner, huddled together like a bunch of flapping little monks.

"Oh, they're such sweeties when they're all cuddly together!" Miss Bates exclaimed. "You know, some vandals spray paint whole bat colonies. How can they? It's beyond me … In fact, I'd love to spray paint those vandals where the sun don't shine!"

"At least they haven't chosen my easel for their roost," Shona's dad said.

"Attics like this are like Heaven to bats," Miss Bates said. "All sorts of nooks and crannies for them to crawl around in and raise a family. We'll leave them to their domestic bliss for now. I'll call Bat Conservation to come and remove them. It's a job for the professionals!"

Then she turned to Shona's dad. "The attic will need a good clean-up afterwards," she said. "Bat wee does not smell good, Garfield, and it might ruin your paintings."

"I can see I've got my work cut out," Shona's dad said. He shook his head at the thought of a clean-up of his precious junk.

While all this was going on, Shona had not dared to go up to the attic. She had been downstairs keeping her granny company.

"Appears we have some squatters in the attic," she heard her dad say, as he came into the living room.

"A whole family," her mum added. "Your dad's so-called memorabilia proved the perfect roosting place."

"Once the hatch is closed," Miss Bates told her, "they won't be a bother. Then it's over to the professionals to remove them to a safe place. They're an endangered species, you know. Anyway, we have this little soul to lay to rest."

Shona saw that her teacher was holding the little bat she'd taken from the airing cupboard.

"Can we bury it by the cat? Then they'll have each other for company," Shona said. They had buried her pet cat at the foot of the rose bush that grew near the fence.

And after her mum had shovelled up a bat-sized hole, Miss Bates laid out the bat.

"Fly in peace, little flitter mouse!" Miss Bates said.

"Gone to a better place, I hope," Granny said when they told her.

"Now that's done, I must love and leave you good people," Miss Bates said. "See you tomorrow, Shona."

With that, off went Miss Bates on her bike.

"She's as crazy as they come," Shona's dad said. "But I bet she's a great teacher. I wish I had a teacher like her in my days."

"Crazy in a nice way," Shona's mum agreed.

Chapter 9
Not One of Us

Next day, Miss Bates announced that she had an idea for a special Halloween assembly.

'Another one of her bright ideas by the sound of it,' Shona thought.

Yes, for Halloween, the class would perform a dance drama. And not just any dance drama. It was going to be a dance drama inspired by a legend about ...

No prizes for guessing …

Bats!

First, Miss Bates divided the class into two groups – A for the animals, B for the birds.

Then she went on to tell them the legend. It was from the Cree people of North America. Miss Bates had adapted it a little.

"One day the animals decide to challenge the birds to a ball game," she said. "A game rather like rugby. The animals were confident they'd run circles round the birds with their paws and teeth.

"'Let me play for your team,' Bat says to the birds.

"'No way José!' Eagle cries. He is captain of the birds' team. 'You might have wings but you're not one of us.'

"And the birds all joined in with, 'You're not one of us!'

"So Bat says to the animals, 'Pick me, please pick me. Have I not got four legs like you lot? Come on, guys, have I not got teeth like you?'

"'You're not one of us!' the animals grunted. 'Don't make us laugh. You and your four legs!

Ha! True, you have two back legs. But just look at your front legs, more like two twitchy little wings with fingers and a thumb. Maybe you should be playing for the humans' team!'

"And the animals erupt into so much laughter they all give themselves stitches.

"'Hang on, not so fast,' Tiger says. He is the captain of the animals' team. 'True, Bat got no teeth to write home about!' Tiger grinned and displayed an impressive set of chompers, just to make his point. 'But Deer's still got a bad leg from a hunter's bullet,' he went on, 'which means we are one short. Look at Bat – what he lacks in talent, he makes up for in effort.'

"It wasn't always wise to disagree with Tiger, and so the rest of the animals said, 'Have it your way, Tiger. Bat can play for our team. Not that he'll be any use!'

"But soon the birds were wishing they'd chosen Bat. With an odd combination of wing-work and teeth-work, he was one mean contender. He gripped the ball with his tiny teeth and flew round the field faster than you could say Usain Bolt.

"And so Bat helped the animals to victory over the birds.

"'That still doesn't make you one of us,' the animals said.

"'And you're certainly not one of us,' said the birds.

"Hurt and disappointed, Bat took himself off to a dark corner of the nearest cave and hung face down. Ever since then, Bat has been hanging upside down ..."

Miss Bates paused. "So what's that legend saying to us?" she asked.

"Is it about gratitude?" Ewa said. "The animals didn't thank Bat for helping them win?"

"That's one way of seeing it, Ewa," Miss Bates said. "But ancient legends are like poems. They work on many levels."

"Is it about fairness?" Shona asked. "All Bat wanted was a fair chance to play and prove his skills."

"Why not, Shona?" Miss Bates said. "That's another way to look at it. But, class, remind me – what do the birds and animals say to Bat as they reject him?"

"You're not one of us!" the whole class shouted.

"Exactly! *You're not one of us!*" Miss Bates beamed. "People love to put others into neat little boxes. Tick, tick, all done and dusted! But Bat doesn't seem to fit into any box. Wings, yet not a bird. Teeth, yet not an animal. A mousey face, yet not a mouse. Sometimes bats are called flying foxes or even flying squirrels. That's enough to keep anyone guessing."

With that, Miss Bates clapped her hands. "And now it's time for some dance and some drama. Give it your best shot! Group A, when you do your animal dance, I expect some good leaps and bounds. Use those legs. Group B, when you do your bird dance, I expect some good flapping and flying. Work those arms."

"Can I be Eagle, captain of the birds' team?" Ewa asked. "I'm good at flapping."

The class laughed and chanted, "Ewa! Ewa! Ewa!"

So Ewa was elected to be Eagle.

"Eagle does a solo dance, so you'll have every chance to show off your flapping, Ewa," Miss Bates said with a grin. "I'll be bossy Tiger in my best stripy onesie. But no laughing at me! All we're missing is our Bat. Any volunteers?"

Silence.

Nobody, it seemed, wanted to be Bat. Nobody wanted to be "not one of us", even if it was only make-believe.

Shona found herself putting her hand in the air.

"Well done, Shona," Miss Bates said. "You've just landed yourself the part of Bat. And since your mum's into drama, I'll expect great things. Embrace your fear and you'll make an excellent Bat."

Chapter 10
Good Luck

Beep beep! Beep beep!

That was Shona making beepy noises around the house.

Beep beep! Beep beep!

"Shona! What are you playing at?" her mum asked.

"Hush!" her dad said. "What is this? Some kind of playground craze?"

"No," Shona explained. "These are my sound effects. Ultra-sounds. Like a bat makes. I've got the part of Bat in Miss Bates's Halloween dance drama."

Her mum and dad smiled at each other. "Ah Miss Bates, we should have guessed," they said.

Granny cracked on with a needle and thread, rigging up a bat costume from shimmery black fabric for Shona to wear over a pair of velvety tights.

Soon Shona was "set for stardom", as her dad put it.

For the next few days, Miss Bates's classroom was a hive of activity, with cardboard and felt and tissue paper and ribbons all to be cut and shaped into animal and bird masks.

As the show got closer, the butterflies in Shona's stomach were getting active.

"Don't worry," her mum said. "It will be all right on the night."

In fact, it was more than all right. The show went down to foot-stomping applause.

Ewa was Eagle, in a fleecy grey hoody with a superb yellow beak. She was in flapping form, leading her team of birds through the audience.

And Shona brought a hush into the room with her spins and flits as she winged through the air in Granny's dark-as-night bat costume. She was indeed a star as she took a bow like a proper bat diva.

As for Miss Bates herself – well, she acted up a storm as bossy Tiger in her stripy black and yellow onesie and matching fluffy slippers. When the moment came for Tiger's solo dance, she broke into a wicked Brazilian samba, combined with some Morris Dancing high kicks that had the audience falling over.

But what Miss Bates hadn't told the class was that the whole performance was being filmed, and a clip would be shown at the My Kind of Teacher award ceremony at the Town Hall.

Yes, Miss Bates had been nominated for an award

Miss Bates smiled and blushed. "I wanted it to be a surprise," she said.

A few days later, the class were at the award ceremony in the Town Hall.

Miss Bates was looking set for stardom. She was all dressed up, more stylish than ever in a slinky black dress and silver high-heels that showed off her toenails painted black like her fingernails. Shona could see the gleam of her bat tattoo on her shoulder.

In her speech, she said that a teacher helps her pupils to discover their own voices, and to be the best they can be.

"This one is for you guys," she said, and she waved the award in the direction of her class.

"This calls for a celebration," Shona's mum and dad said afterwards when they at last got to congratulate Miss Bates.

"I've got some good news too," Shona's mum said. "My agent rang to tell me I've landed the part of the Snow Queen."

"Brilliant," said Miss Bates, and she gave her a hug.

Then Shona's mum said, "Shall I share your good news, Garfield, or will you?"

All of a sudden, Shona's dad went all shy.

"One of his paintings has been selected for the Royal Academy Summer Exhibition next year!" Shona said.

"Brilliant," said Miss Bates again, and she gave him a big hug too.

Time flew past until it was December.

On the first night of Mum's Snow Queen panto, Shona's granny couldn't believe her eyes when the December skies pelted down flurries of snow that transformed houses into white wedding cakes and parks into skating rinks.

"About time!" she sighed. "This white Christmas long overdue. Where's that son of mine? Come quick, Garfield, bring the camera. I want a photo in the snow to send back to the folks-dem in Montserrat."

Shona's dad turned to Shona's mum and said, "Remember what Miss Bates told us about how the Chinese believe bats bring good luck?

Well, looks like the bats in the attic brought us all a share of good luck."

"The Chinese might be on to something," Shona's mum said.

Shona looked out the window at the snow and smiled. "Serendipity," was all she said.

"Serendipity," she repeated, loving the sound of the word, and thinking how the more you get to know people the harder it is to put them in boxes and label them.

A bit like bats really.